ROHINI'S DIARY

AN ADULT FAIRY TALE

ANOUSHKA
CHAKRABORTY

Copyright © Anoushka Chakraborty
All Rights Reserved.

This book has been self-published with all reasonable efforts taken to make the material error-free by the author. No part of this book shall be used, reproduced in any manner whatsoever without written permission from the author, except in the case of brief quotations embodied in critical articles and reviews.

The Author of this book is solely responsible and liable for its content including but not limited to the views, representations, descriptions, statements, information, opinions and references ["Content"]. The Content of this book shall not constitute or be construed or deemed to reflect the opinion or expression of the Publisher or Editor. Neither the Publisher nor Editor endorse or approve the Content of this book or guarantee the reliability, accuracy or completeness of the Content published herein and do not make any representations or warranties of any kind, express or implied, including but not limited to the implied warranties of merchantability, fitness for a particular purpose. The Publisher and Editor shall not be liable whatsoever for any errors, omissions, whether such errors or omissions result from negligence, accident, or any other cause or claims for loss or damages of any kind, including without limitation, indirect or consequential loss or damage arising out of use, inability to use, or about the reliability, accuracy or sufficiency of the information contained in this book.

Made with ♥ on the Notion Press Platform
www.notionpress.com

To Me

To All of us

Contents

Foreword

In a world where fairy tales are often sanitized, this book delves into a realm where magic meets maturity, and fantasy mingles with reality. These are not the fairy tales you heard as a child; they are stories for adults who seek enchantment with a touch of complexity. Here, characters grapple with passion, desire, and the consequences of their choices. The enchanted forests are darker, the spells more potent, and the journeys more intense. This collection invites you to rediscover classic themes through a new, bold lens—where the happily ever after is earned, not just wished for. Well you won't get any magic realism here...

Preface

Welcome to the realm of Rohini's Diary, where reality blurs and dreams take flight.

In the hustle and bustle of our daily lives, it's easy to become ensnared in the mundane routines and obligations that tether us to the world. But within the pages of this book lies an invitation to break free from the shackles of reality and embark on a journey of enchantment and escape.

As you turn the pages, you'll be transported to worlds both familiar and fantastical, where ordinary lives collide with extraordinary circumstances. Here, the constraints of time and space fade away, and the boundaries between the possible and the impossible blur into oblivion.

This book is not merely a collection of words on paper; it is a portal to realms unknown—a passport to the farthest reaches of the human imagination. Within these pages, you'll find the journey of Rohini, a simple girl whose life turns an expected turn.

But remember, dear reader, that while the landscapes may be fantastical, the emotions they evoke are all too real. For it is in the realm of fiction that we confront the truths of our own existence most directly, cloaked in the guise of make-believe.

So let go of your worries, set aside your troubles, and allow yourself to be swept away by the currents of imagination. For in the world of fiction, anything is possible—and the only limit is the boundaries of your own mind.

With warmest regards and sincerest wishes for an unforgettable journey,

PREFACE

Here's to those who find solace amidst the peaks of mountains and the pages of books. To the sanctuary seekers, may your journey through the realms of knowledge and nature be as fulfilling as the ascent to the highest summit. Cheers to the adventures of university life, where every lesson learned and every peak conquered shapes our futures.

Acknowledgements

Thank you life

Prologue

In the heart of winter, as the news whispers of snow near Tiger Hills, I find myself nestled with Rohini's Diary. Friendships from university often weave a tapestry stronger than family bonds. As a close observer of her journey, I decide to unlock the secrets held within those pages, contemplating the possibility of sharing these tales. The chill in the air outside contrasts with the warmth of memories awaiting discovery within the diary's covers. And so, with a coffee mug in hand, I embark on a journey through the chronicles of Rohini's life.

ONE

JANEMAAN IT'S JANUARY

So, here's the lowdown on my life in Ranipur. I'm Rohini Chattopadhyay, 23, knee-deep in my postgrad mess, and wrestling with my parents' drama. Right now, I'm stuck in Ranipur for the cultural fiesta that goes down every January. Ever heard of Peterson Hills? It's like my chill spot near Darjeeling, and I'm bouncing over there soon to escape the chaos.

Oh, and guess what? I'm your friendly neighborhood dancer, specializing in Bharatnatyam. Need a stage show? Just hit me up – I'm just a call away. My parents? Yeah, they're in their own world, and honestly, I've got better things to do than deal with their vibes.

Decided to spice up my diary game. Instead of the usual drab entries, I'm dropping monthly summaries. Flashback to the end of 2022 – my boyfriend, Anupam, turned out to be Mr. Unfaithful. New year, new heartbreak, right? But hey, let's not dwell.

Rolling into 2023, it's like a dance-off between heartbreak and optimism. January's all about these cultural shindigs, my personal therapy sessions. Music and dance are my saving grace, helping me shake off the drama from last year.

Parents on the backburner, I'm embracing Peterson Hills soon. January might have kicked off with betrayal, but it's turning into this canvas for rediscovery. Life's a mixtape of pain and joy, and I'm just trying to find the sweet spots.

So, that's the scoop from my side of the hill. Here's to hoping the next chapter brings more dance, less drama, and maybe a bit of sunshine on the horizon. Cheers to a vibe-filled 2023!

TWO
FEBRUARY FAIRYTALES

February burst onto the scene with the grandeur of Mumma and Papa's anniversary – a spectacle of love, or as I like to call it, an oxymoron at its absolute peak. They decided to mark the occasion with a celebration at home, probably involving more romance than I could fathom. Meanwhile, here I am, tackling the complexities of life at Peterson Hills University.

The university experience is a wild ride, but the real plot twist is the eclectic bunch of friends I've gathered along the way. Anoushka, Vishal, Rohit, Firdausi – it's like assembling the Avengers, only with a lot more laughter and fewer superpowers. They've become the support system I never knew I needed.

Then there's Rahaat, the resident oddball in our class. Always surrounded by a gaggle of girls, he's like a magnet for drama. Me? I prefer to keep a safe distance, steering clear of his orbit of chaos. I've got my own universe to navigate, thank you very much.

Speaking of navigating, I recently moved into a new apartment, bidding farewell to my old PG life. The best part? This place allows guys, and enter Anupam – my anchor in the storm of academia. Moving in with him feels like a step towards adulthood, even if we still indulge in late-night snack runs and binge-watch our favorite shows.

The new apartment is more than just a change of address; it's a sanctuary. No more cramped spaces and shared bathrooms. Now, I have the luxury of solitude for my dance practice. The rhythm of my feet against the floor blends seamlessly with the peaceful silence, creating an ambiance that's nothing short of poetic. It's in these moments that I find inspiration to pour my heart out onto paper, penning verses that capture the essence of my journey.

Amidst all this, Anupam and I hit a rough patch. Long-distance relationships are like walking a tightrope, and we stumbled. There was a glitch, a moment of weakness that led to accusations of cheating. The air was thick with tension, and it felt like our four-year-long connection was hanging by a thread.

But then came the apology – sincere, raw, and laden with the weight of realization. It was a glitch, not a betrayal. Our love, tested and tried, emerged stronger. February, the month of love, had thrown us a curveball, but we caught it together. Life is messy, love is messier, but it's these twists and turns that make the journey worthwhile.

As the days unfold in Peterson Hills, I find myself embracing the chaos of university life, savoring the moments of laughter with friends, navigating the dance of relationships, and finding solace in the stillness of my apartment. Love, in all its forms, is a constant companion on this rollercoaster ride, and I wouldn't have it any other way. After all, isn't the beauty of life in its unpredictability?

Guess who rolled into town just in time for Valentine's Day? Anupam, straight from the heart of Delhi. Forget the roses and chocolates; his arrival was the sweetest surprise.

As we caught up, dreams of a future together danced in my head. We strolled down the streets of Peterson Hills, hand in hand, making plans that involved more than just textbooks and deadlines. Anupam brought a slice of Delhi with him – the chaos, the energy, and that unmistakable Delhi vibe.

Valentine's Day was a celebration of us, the mismatched yet perfectly synced duo. No grand gestures, just the simple joy of being together. We traded heartfelt laughter, shared secrets, and maybe indulged in a bit too much chocolate.

In the midst of it all, we dared to dream. Anupam's visit became a canvas for painting our future, sketching the contours of a life where "us" triumphed over everything else. Peterson Hills witnessed our love story unfold, with Valentine's Day marking a chapter filled with warmth, laughter, and the promise of more adventures to come. Love, it turns out, is the best kind of celebration.

February to me is like a literary ruckus, blending triumphs and personal complexities into one wild ride. First up, my babies – the books I'd poured my heart into – made their debut at the Kolkata Book Fair. Seeing them on display was like a proud parent moment, except my kids were made of paper and ink. Creative endeavors turned tangible, and I basked in the glow of literary accomplishment.

Then, fate decided to play matchmaker during a viva exam. Rahaat, the campus oddball, popped up like a character from a sitcom. Academic pursuits collided with the unpredictable, adding an unexpected layer to the month. Who knew a viva could be a rendezvous with sitcom-level drama?

Now, let's talk about the real soap opera – my love life. Anupam, my long-distance anchor, got a front-row seat to the mess. Baseless doubts about Rahaat crept in, casting shadows on my interactions. In a loyalty-driven decision, I hit the block button, shutting down a potential plot twist with Rahaat. It was a move to keep the peace, but man, love can be as complicated as a Netflix series plot.

University days, though, were a saving grace in this chaos. The four walls of lecture halls witnessed friendships blooming, inside jokes forming, and the occasional napping during boring lectures. The struggle was real, but the camaraderie made it worthwhile. Ah, the joys of surviving on instant noodles and 2 AM study sessions – university life, you're a wild ride.

Back to the tumultuous currents of personal relationships. Despite the doubts and the occasional emotional storms, February unfolded with the grace of an approaching spring. The literary victories and academic milestones painted the canvas of the month in hues of accomplishment. Life surged ahead, and I embraced the ebb and flow, recognizing that amidst complexities, the beauty of each moment propels us forward.

In the chaos, there's a realization that life isn't a neatly scripted movie; it's a messy, unedited documentary. And you know what? That's what makes it interesting. Each day became a page in this evolving story – a story that I was writing as I went along. The unpredictability, the challenges, the triumphs – they all added flavor to the narrative.

In the grand scheme of things, love isn't a perfectly curated Instagram feed. It's messy hair, unplanned adventures, and yes, occasionally blocking someone for the sake of sanity. It's Anupam, the guy who traveled from Delhi to be there for Valentine's Day, understanding the chaos and being a part of the unfiltered, unedited version of my life.

As February embraced me in its whirlwind, I found solace in the approaching spring. The metaphor wasn't lost on me – just like the promise of blooming flowers, every complex moment held the potential for growth. Life was a journey, and each encounter, each twist, added a layer to the tapestry of experiences.

So, here I am, embracing the chaos, riding the waves of university life, love, creative pursuits. February, with all its madness, became a chapter in the book of my life – a chapter that made me laugh, cry, and appreciate the messy beauty of it all. After all, who needs a perfectly scripted story when you can have an adventure?

THREE

MEMORIES OF MARCH

So, March hits me like a wrecking ball, and not the Miley Cyrus kind. Picture this: I end up in this crazy accident, and bam, my face is like a Picasso painting gone wrong. It's a total horror show, and the mirror becomes this daily horror movie.

Guess what? Only Vishal's got the backstage pass to the real drama. Anupam, my supposed buddy, throws three punches my way after a little spat. And my folks? Clueless and chilling like it's just another day in paradise.

Acceptance? Yeah, right. Trying to make peace with this new face in the mirror is like negotiating with a stubborn toddler. It's not just about the scars; it's this whole identity crisis that comes with it. Mirror me is playing mind games, and I'm just trying to keep up.

Decision time: pack my bags and head to Kolkata for a makeover, not the fashion kind. But here's the catch – it's a one-way ticket away from my cozy academic bubble. University life? Sayonara. Now, it's all about rehab and figuring out who I am post-punch fest.

No more lectures, no familiar faces, just me in this void that used to be my university life. The corridors that once buzzed with academic banter are now silent reminders of the interruption that is my life.

But hold up, in the midst of this gloom, guess what decides to sprout? Resilience, my friend. Kolkata turns out to be more than just a pitstop for medical touch-ups. It's like this boot camp for strength and endurance. Every step toward recovery is a mic-drop moment for the human spirit.

March is playing this crazy symphony of fear and pain, but I'm rocking the determined footsteps toward healing. The journey is a rollercoaster, but there's this subtle promise that even when life throws shade, you can rebuild and find solace in the chaos.

The streets of Kolkata become my new hangout spot. The markets, the colors, the people – it's all therapy. Yeah, the medical stuff is happening, but the real challenge is facing those deep, existential questions. Who am I now, with this face? Kolkata becomes my canvas to figure that out.

Surrounded by strangers, I find comfort in the anonymity. The city doesn't care about my scars or my past. It's like the cool friend who accepts you, flaws and all. It's my healing haven, where I can rebuild without the judgment.

Days blur into a routine of appointments, therapy, and solo strolls. The Ganges becomes my silent therapist, witnessing my struggles. Each ripple in the river feels like an echo of the resilience I'm uncovering in myself.

As the physical wounds slowly fade, the emotional scars linger. The mirror still throws me this weird look, but I'm learning to throw a smile back. Kolkata teaches me that acceptance isn't about erasing scars; it's about rocking them with pride.

Without lectures and textbooks, life becomes the real classroom. Lessons unfold in the chaos of the streets, the random chats with strangers, and the quiet moments by the river. Kolkata, with its contradictions, becomes a mirror to my own journey – chaotic yet harmonious, ancient yet evolving.

Support comes from unexpected corners, adding color to this grayscale phase. Strangers become allies, and the city becomes my collective therapist. March nears its end, and the echoes of fear and pain fade. In their place, this newfound strength resonates. The journey, initially an escape, transforms into a self-discovery trip.

Heading back home is like a movie ending. The faces, the corridors – they're familiar, but I'm not the same. The scars are now part of my story. My parents, still in the dark, see a changed but resilient version of their kid.

March, with its crazy twists, becomes a game-changer. It's not just pain; it's a saga of resilience, self-discovery, and embracing the chaos. Kolkata, with its wild energy, is the unsung hero of this transformation. The city's spirit blends with mine, leaving an indelible mark on my healing journey.

Now, when I face the mirror, it's not a horror show. The reflection doesn't freak me out; it reflects the strength and courage born from that unexpected March madness. The scars? They're not just reminders of pain; they're badges of survival. Kolkata didn't just fix my face; it stitched together a kickass new chapter—one that wears scars like battle scars, stories of resilience and a journey well-fought.I'm chilling far from the university scene, posted up in Ranipur. Vishal's my info lifeline, shooting notes my way. But the whole "get back to university ASAP" vibe? Nah, not my jam. Lost the urge, lost the connections. Ranipur's got me in a different zone, and that academic routine? It's not pulling me back. Vishal's doing his update thing, but the campus life? Feels like a distant memory.

Maybe it's the Ranipur vibes or just a detour I'm cool with. University's on pause, and I'm in no rush to hit play.

FOUR

APRIL IS THE CRUELEST MONTH

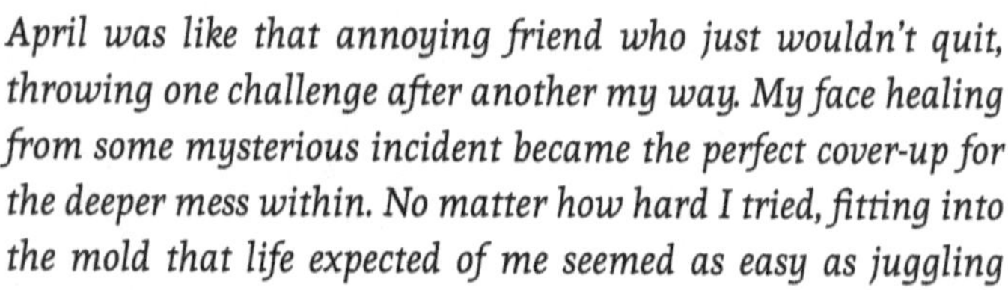

April was like that annoying friend who just wouldn't quit, throwing one challenge after another my way. My face healing from some mysterious incident became the perfect cover-up for the deeper mess within. No matter how hard I tried, fitting into the mold that life expected of me seemed as easy as juggling flaming chainsaws.

My parents, despite my superhero efforts in academics and daily life, remained perpetually unsatisfied. It's like they had an ever-growing list of expectations, and I was always falling short. Meanwhile, Anupam and his Sherlock Holmes-level gaslighting skills were turning our relationship into a crime scene. The suspicion that he might be pulling some undercover operation of infidelity added a spicy layer to my silent struggles.

Stuck in this weird limbo between wanting to break free and the shackles of society's expectations, I felt like a deer caught in headlights. An open relationship with Anupam and the oh-so-prestigious family background created this suffocating atmosphere. Fear of judgment and the horror of tarnishing the family name kept me shackled to a relationship that was slowly sucking the life out of me.

Day by day, the weight of these issues pushed me further down the rabbit hole of depression. Devastation became my BFF, and in a desperate attempt to escape reality, I found solace in the numbing embrace of weed and some questionable substances. Yeah, it was a risky move, but in the chaos of my life, it seemed like the only way to keep my sanity afloat.

So, I finally roll back into Peterson Hills, expecting some sort of homey comfort. Surprise, surprise! My friends suddenly turned into silent ninjas. University life became a confusing maze with attendance dropping faster than my hopes of a drama-free existence. And, of course, I patched things up with Anupam because, let's face it, I can't survive without him. He might have a temper issue, but that bruised face of mine? Just a result of a not-so-friendly accident.

Oh, and Vishal and I? Well, let's just say our friendship hit a speed bump when he couldn't wrap his head around my genius decision of getting back with Mr. Short-Temper.

Rahaat? Who knows? Probably off having adventures in Narnia or something.

In the midst of pretending everything was picture-perfect for the sake of society, I was basically a hot mess internally. April, which was supposed to be all about healing, turned into a battleground for my sanity. It's like my life was a sitcom, and someone forgot to give me the script.

FIVE
MAY MANIA

It's my BirthMonth, and the 25th of May is looming, marking the beginning of my 24th journey around the sun. The question echoes in my mind: should I part ways with Anupam after a four-year relationship or endure a bit more? He has been my sanctuary, an escape from the clutches of my toxic parents whose inflictions from my childhood linger like stubborn ghosts.

Nausea has become an unwelcome companion, prompting me to consider a visit to the doctor. As the days roll by, the anticipation for my birthday dwindles, replaced by an impending sense of dread. Anupam's sudden decision to block me on the 16th, following a trivial fight, shatters my world. The universe's hints become a deafening reality – he won't unblock me, and it's the end.

Emotionally ravaged, I meet Rahaat at the university a day before my birthday. The conversation lasts a mere two to four minutes, devoid of any special significance. Tension lingers as I realize my periods are MIA for the past two months, adding another layer of uncertainty to my tumultuous life.

On the 25th, my birthday arrives, and I travel to my hometown, Ranipur, determined to celebrate in my own way. I adorn myself in a knee-length, deep-necked black dress – a rebellious choice against Anupam's restrictions. The celebration is grand, a temporary escape from the harsh realities that await my return to Peterson Hills.

Back at the university, I muster the courage to confront the truth through a pregnancy test. The result is a seismic revelation – I'm pregnant. Anupam, the one person I thought I could lean on, remains silent, rejecting my calls. The echoes of my emotional turmoil reverberate in the silence of unanswered calls and the reality of an unexpected pregnancy.

As I stand on the precipice of a new age, the road ahead is uncertain. Shattered love, parental scars, and the impending responsibilities of motherhood form a complex tapestry. The weight of my decisions bears down on me, and the question of whether to continue this journey alone or with Anupam remains unanswered.

So, 27th May rolled around, and I found myself at Anoushka's birthday bash – you know, the usual deal with friends from the university, good food, and some human touches. Frankly, I was there because the thought of cooking made me shudder. Why slave over a stove when Anoushka's place promised a feast?

Now, here I am, navigating post-breakup life, holding down a job with a decent paycheck. Oh, and did I mention I'm on the Bollywood track? Yep, I chose to keep the baby, embrace the whole "raise him or her" saga. Call it filmy, call it crazy – I'm just being a Bollywood girl in this unpredictable script of life.

Lo and behold, Rahaat makes a reappearance at the birthday bonanza. Yep, I unblocked him post-breakup because, well, why not add a little twist to the plot? We ended up having a chat, sharing our food like it was some kind of intimate culinary exchange. Random cute things started happening, you know, the kind that make you question if life is just a series of serendipitous moments strung together....And Anoushka walks *in*

Me: Hey Anoushka! Happy birthday, you beauty with brain. Another year wiser, huh?

Anoushka: Thanks a ton! Wise or not, I'm just thrilled to have awesome people like you around.

Rahaat: Well, well, look who's the birthday star! Anoushka, you dazzle more than these party lights tonight.

Me: Smooth, Rahaat. Real smooth. Anoushka, this guy's a pro at compliments.

*Anoushka: *laughs* I can tell. Thanks, Rahaat, and thanks, you two, for making my day already.*

Rahaat: It's your day, Anoushka. Anything special you're looking forward to?

Anoushka: Hmm, just good times, good company, and maybe a few surprises. By the way, did you bring any surprises, you sneaky pair?

Me: Surprises? Well, let's just say the night is young, and the surprises might just unfold.

*Rahaat: *winks* Who knows what the night holds? Anoushka, any favorite birthday memories so far?*

Anoushka: Oh, loads of them. But honestly, every year brings something new and exciting. Speaking of exciting, any plans for the night?

Me: Well, besides devouring this amazing spread you've got here, maybe a dance or two. Rahaat, you up for a dance?

Rahaat: Absolutely! I've been waiting for the perfect dance partner, and what better night than tonight?

Anoushka: Count me in too! Let's make it a trio.

*Me: Trio it is! *raises a glass* To good food, great company, and the most fantastic birthday girl.*

*Anoushka: *clinks glasses* Cheers to that! By the way, Rahaat, how did you manage to get these two lovely ladies as your dance partners?*

Rahaat: Oh, it's a secret skill I possess. It's called charm.

Me: *laughs* Watch out, Anoushka, we've got a charmer in our midst.

Anoushka: Well, I'm not complaining. Let the charming commence!

Rahaat: To the dance floor, then! *leads the way

As Anoushka left to greet other guests, we continued with laughter, dancing, and the kind of casual banter that makes memories. The birthday celebration became a laid-back affair, still filled with spontaneous conversations and the promise of more joy in the moments yet to come.In these chatter and laughter, Rahaat, with that charming smile of his, suggests a friendly long drive. Now, I'm no stranger to spontaneity, so I said yes. A long drive – a simple, friendly escapade, just what I needed. Of course, I'm fully aware of my limits; after all, I'm carrying a little secret within. Pregnancy hormones and all, but who says you can't enjoy a friendly long drive without going overboard?

As we hit the road, the conversation flows effortlessly. We share stories, jokes, and a playlist that somehow caters to both our tastes. The city lights become a mesmerizing backdrop to our impromptu adventure, and the hum of the engine provides the soundtrack to this casual escapade.

Somewhere along the drive, Rahaat reaches for my hand. It's not a grand gesture, just a simple intertwining of fingers. Yet, in that moment, it speaks volumes. The night air is filled with the hum of the engine, shared laughter, and the promise of something new.

We return, the friendly long drive etched into the diary of memories. It might not be a grand love story or a dramatic Bollywood script, but it's our little chapter – filled with random cuteness, shared food, and the understanding that life, despite its unpredictability, can still surprise you in the most delightful *ways.*

In the haze of emotions, I grapple with the tangled threads of my life. The toxic tendrils of my past intertwine with the newfound challenges of the future. 31ˢᵗ Night, the air thick with anticipation and the aroma of weed. Unsteady but resolute, I dialed Rahaat's number after three or four puffs, my mind clouded by intoxication but oddly content with the life growing within.

Me: Hey, Rahaat! You won't believe what's up.

Rahaat: Oh, hey! What's going on? You sound... different.

Me: Different is good, right? Guess what? I'm pregnant.

Rahaat: (stunned silence) Wait, what? Pregnant? Are you serious?

Me: Totally serious. Life's throwing surprises, and I'm rolling with it. It's a wild ride, my friend.

Rahaat: (nervously chuckled)Wow, that's... unexpected. How are you feeling about it?

Me: Feeling? I'm feeling like I'm on cloud nine, Rahaat! It's like this crazy mix of emotions – scared, excited, and a bit wobbly from the weed.

Rahaat: I... I didn't see this coming. Have you talked to Anupam about it?

Me: Anupam? Nah, he's off the radar, blocked my calls and all. But you, my dear friend, get the exclusive. Aren't you thrilled?

Rahaat: Thrilled, shocked, a bit of both. It's a lot to take in. Are you sure about this?

*Me: * Sure? Who's ever sure about anything? But hey, life's short, and this little nugget inside me is a game-changer.*

Rahaat: It's just... unexpected. And you're not in the best state right now, you know? Intoxication and all.

*Me: * Best state? Who defines that anyway? I'm happy, Rahaat. This little revelation is making my night unforgettable.*

Rahaat: I'm happy for you, really. It's just, I didn't expect to hear this tonight.

Me: Life's full of surprises, my friend. Embrace the chaos! And hey, you're in for some babysitting duty once this little munchkin arrives.

Rahaat: (laughs) Babysitting duty? I'll cross that bridge when we get there. For now, let's enjoy the craziness of tonight.

Me: Cheers to that, Rahaat! Life's one wild journey, and I'm strapped in for the ride. (And I take another puff)

The conversation unfolds in the haze of intoxication and unexpected news, a snapshot of a pivotal moment in the unpredictable narrative of my life.

SIX

SIX

JUNE E JAHANNUM

*It's friggin' June, and guess what? It's your girl, Rohini Chattopadhyay, and I'm knee-deep in my very own "R**dy-Rona" saga. Postgrad life at Peterson Hill University? More like a never-ending nightmare. Parents? Toxic AF. Anupam? Dumped me. Pregnant? Like, who gives a damn?*

I'm pulling all-nighters for exams, dragging my sorry self to night shifts at JWU Industries. University? It's a judgmental circus, with everyone giving me the stink-eye. Alone, pregnant, and drowning in the sea of everyone's disapproval – it's a whole damn mess.

So, what's my escape? Weed, my constant companion, and that favorite whiskey that's become my BFF. I'm sprawled on my bed, surrounded by the swirling smoke, trying to find some peace in this chaos. But peace? Where the heck is it? Facing my pregnancy journey solo? I'm clueless, and the university's icy silence only adds to the devastation.

As June unfolds, I'm hanging onto the threads of routine – exams, night shifts – and numbing myself with the hazy embrace of substances. The room spins, and I'm lost in this messed-up reality.Thoughts of raising a child alone feels like an impending disaster, and the loneliness is suffocating. The university, once a place of hope, is now a cold, heartless dungeon.

Summer break in the hills, like, why? Everyone's back, and there's Rahaat, ringing me up all the time. Dude, show up already! I'm in this weird mood, can't decide if I wanna chat with him or not. It's like, "Rahaat, buddy, where you hiding?" Feeling all fuzzy and floaty, you know? Can't figure out if I'm in the mood or not. These hills, man, messing with my head. Rahaat, if you're around, help me out of this tipsy haze. Phones buzzing, and I'm like, "To answer or not?" Life in the hills — confusing, but kinda cool. Here's to the summery daze and maybe, just maybe, a chill chat with Rahaat.

Ugh, this diary thing is like, so not my vibe right now. I'd rather be with my whiskey glass, you know? It's like my BFF tonight. Who needs to write when there's this golden liquid magic? Not me, for sure! Cheers to the whiskey and a night of way better things than diaries.

*In the midst of my intoxicated stupor, I'm desperately trying to piece together the shattered parts of my life. Weed and whiskey are my sorry crutches in this booze-soaked, smoke-filled tragedy. The haze is my only escape from the devastation, a brief respite from the relentless "R**dy-Rona" that echoes in the emptiness of my messed-up world.*

SEVEN

JULY: JUGGLING EMOTIONS

It's the 10th of July, and let me tell you, the stress of upcoming exams is hitting me like a ton of bricks. I'm Rohini Chattopadhyay, just your average university student trying to survive the academic jungle. But here's the kicker – there's a secret I've been juggling. I'm four months pregnant, and guess what? Only my ride-or-die, Rahaat, knows about it.

Now, picture this: I'm trying to keep this baby news on the down-low, but my not-so-little bump is out there for everyone to see. Cue the wild speculations from my fellow students. Thank the universe for Rahaat, though. He's keeping my intoxication habits in check and being the rock I need right now.

Oh, and then there's Anupam, a significant character in my soap opera. He dropped a bomb on me a week ago – living in bliss with his colleague and accusing me of juggling multiple relationships. Like, seriously? He even questioned the paternity of my little one. That hit me hard because, hey, this kid's not some love-child from a crazy fling. I silently promised myself I'd be both mom and dad to this little munchkin.

So, Rahaat and I have this routine. Every evening, he's there, taking me to check-ups, being the support system I never knew I needed. It's smooth sailing, almost dreamy, despite the flying rumors about us. But hey, I made a pact with myself – no falling in love again. Rahaat is strictly in the friend zone.

Now, let's talk about this rainy afternoon – the first real downpour of the monsoon. Rahaat is hanging out at my place, and, well, we made a colossal mistake.

So, there we were, just chilling with our cups of tea and some cookies. Me, all casual and candid, trying to soak in the happy vibes. And then there's Rahaat, being his usual happy and flirtatious self.

I'm like, "You know, Rahaat, these cookies are the real MVPs. They make everything better."

He smirks, "Well, almost everything. I'd say good company makes things even better."

We're bantering back and forth, sipping tea, and laughing like we always do. The atmosphere is so light, and I'm genuinely enjoying the moment. Rahaat's charm is hard to resist, though.

He leans in, raising an eyebrow, "You've got a smile that can light up the whole room, you know that?"

I chuckle, "Flattery will get you everywhere, Rahaat."

And then, out of nowhere, we lock eyes. The energy in the room shifts, and before we know it, we're both leaning in for a kiss. The casual banter turns into something more, and next thing I know, we're swept up in the heat of the moment, cups of tea long forgotten.

It's wild how a friendly conversation over tea and cookies can take such an unexpected turn. But hey, life's full of surprises, right?

So, after that unexpected turn of events, Rahaat drops the bomb, "It's not going to ruin our friendship, right?" And just like that, it became our daily routine – the friendly banter followed by, well, you know.

Now, let's talk about the chaos during exams. Viva day rolls around, and I'm there dealing with some unexpected pregnancy symptoms – hello, nose bleeding. I ring up Rahaat, not spilling the health beans, but he's a no-show. Managed to drag myself to the university, only to find him acting all distant, busy chatting up other girls. Like, seriously? It hit differently. I mean, we're just friends, no strings attached, but damn, it stung.

In the midst of all this, I can't shake the feeling that Rahaat's odd vibes are getting to me. I haven't confronted him about it, and that adds to the dilemma. It's like I signed up for this casual friendship, but now there's this unspoken complexity, and I can't figure out why his actions are affecting me so much. It's a head-scratcher, a mix of emotions, and I'm left wondering why this seemingly straightforward connection suddenly feels like a tangled mess.

Out of the blue, I decide to ditch Peterson Hill, kiss my studies goodbye, and hello Kolkata – because why not, right? The dilemma is real though. Rahaat's odd behavior post our daily rendezvous, the sudden move – it's a rollercoaster of confusion and mixed emotions. I don't even bother asking him about the weird vibes. Instead, I drop the bomb that I'm heading home, maybe not to return. Life's messy, my friend, and so is my casual, complicated friendship with Rahaat. Sleep eluded me that night as I meticulously outlined my agenda for the days ahead. With a touch of cinematic flair, I resolved to make one last visit to Ranipur. Call it filmy, if you will. There's something poetic about embracing the allure of nostalgia before forging into the future.

So, Rahaat shows up like it's just another day, and I play along, pretending yesterday never happened. He whips up my favorite Khichuri and Alubhaja – a last hurrah, maybe. We cuddle, soaking in the normalcy, though it might be our finale.

As he's heading out, I casually drop the bomb about me leaving. You know, just throw it into the mix like it's just another spice in the kitchen. The air gets heavy, filled with unspoken stuff, mixing with the scent of our final shared meal. Life's weird, isn't it?

I: Rahaat, there's something I need to share with you. I'm about to leave, and I might not come back.

Rahaat: (visibly shocked) Leave? Why? What's happening, and why are you dropping this bombshell on me?

I: (emotionally) It's tearing me apart, Rahaat. I don't have all the answers; it's just this overwhelming feeling pushing me away.

Rahaat: (teary-eyed) You can't just leave me in the dark like this. Please, help me understand. What's going on?

I: (heartfelt) I wish I could, Rahaat. It's not about you; it's this inner turmoil that I can't ignore. I'm just as lost as you are.

Rahaat: (emotionally torn) This is so sudden, and it hurts. Can't you reconsider? We've been through so much together.

I: (with a heavy heart) I appreciate your love and friendship, Rahaat, but I can't provide the clarity you're seeking. I need to go.

Rahaat left my place, tears streaming down his face. That night, emotions hung in the air like a heavy storm. The next morning, as I left Peterson Hills, it felt like bidding farewell to a part of my soul, and the permanence of it echoed in the silence.

EIGHT

AWE(SOME/FULL) AUGUST

Umm, like, Kolkata, right? Packed my bags, chatted with the JWU Industries big shots, and bam, corporate life from 9 to 7. Total upgrade from my work-from-home routine. Hello, salary boost and adulting vibes!

And nope, this ain't a Bollywood flick—it's more like a rollercoaster. Dealing with all this stuff is legit hard. But guess what? Jenny, my ride-or-die, is with me 24/7. Did I forget to mention her earlier? Oops!

Jenny, my first cousin, and my awesome uncle and aunty became my fam after mine kinda ghosted me when they heard about my bun in the oven. Life, right?

Peterson Hills? That's in the rearview mirror now. But hold up, I gotta wrap up my degree. Third semester at university is calling my name, and I need those class updates. But calling Vishal? Major courage fail.

And Rahaat? Nope, not happening. Awkward city. Anupam totally called out my not-so-acceptable feelings towards him. Like, what's he up to anyway? His vibes sometimes bring me down, but then I'm like, who cares? Let the devil deal with it!

Thank the stars for Jenny, though. She's my personal cheerleader, turning my frowns into emojis. In this whirlwind of jobs, family drama, and complicated crushes, Jenny's my go-to for laughs, girl talks, and surviving this crazy ride.

No one's really shedding tears for me back in Peterson Hills. And Rahaat? Back to his flirtatious Casanova life, no surprises there. So, I braved it and finally called Anoushka.

Me: Anoushka! Long time, no talk. Guess what? Life's turned into this crazy soap opera.

Anoushka: Whoa, spill the tea! What's going on?

Me: Packed my bags, landed a gig in Kolkata, and guess who's adulting now?

Anoushka: Shut up! Kolkata? Job? You're giving me whiplash. Details, now!

Me: Family drama, pregnancy bomb, you name it. Anyway, how's university treating you?

Anoushka: Hold on, rewind. Pregnancy? What? And uni's a rollercoaster, but I need more on the pregnancy thing!

Me: Yeah, long story. By the way, any chance you have those class notes I desperately need?

Anoushka: Notes later. Back to the drama.

Me: Right? But zip it—no blabbing until I show up in Peterson Hills in December. Promise?

Anoushka: Cross my heart. Your drama is safe with me. Oh, by the way, Rahaat seems pretty restless.

Me: Wait, what? Restless Rahaat? Spill, Anoushka!

Anoushka: Seriously! He's been asking about you, seems kinda sad and numb. Total plot twist.

Me: No way! I thought he was back to his Casanova ways. What's going on with him?

Anoushka: That's the mystery. Something's eating at him, and he's not his usual self.

Me: Weird. I never thought he'd be the restless type. Wonder if it has anything to do with me leaving.

Anoushka: Maybe. He did seem genuinely concerned about you, though. Life's turned into a drama series, huh?

Me: Tell me about it. Well, thanks for the Rahaat update. This whole thing just got even more complicated.

Anoushka: Drama aside, take care of yourself in Kolkata. And spill more details next time—we've got some catching up to do!

So, after that crazy day, I dived headfirst into office chaos, you know? But seriously, who needs more drama? I straight-up ghosted my university peeps—for the sake of my sanity, obviously! Mental peace over complexities, always. Don't have enough time to fill the pages up. Office vibes became my escape, and I'm low-key mastering the art of adulting, or so I tell myself. No more calls to the university crew; let's keep it simple and drama-free. Work, chill, repeat—my kind of mantra.

NINE

SASSY SEPTEMBER

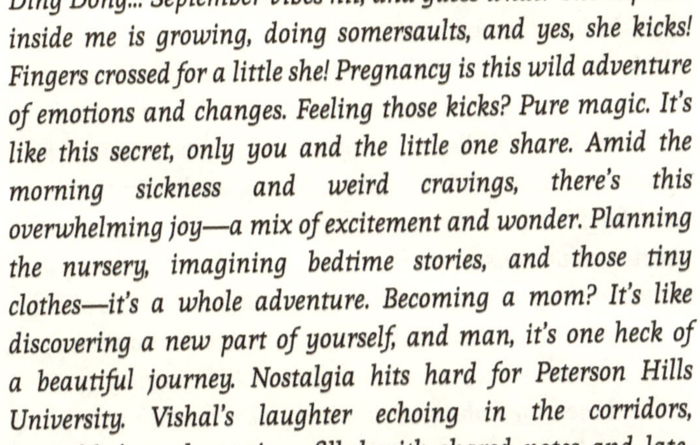

Ding Dong... September vibes hit, and guess what? The cupcake inside me is growing, doing somersaults, and yes, she kicks! Fingers crossed for a little she! Pregnancy is this wild adventure of emotions and changes. Feeling those kicks? Pure magic. It's like this secret, only you and the little one share. Amid the morning sickness and weird cravings, there's this overwhelming joy—a mix of excitement and wonder. Planning the nursery, imagining bedtime stories, and those tiny clothes—it's a whole adventure. Becoming a mom? It's like discovering a new part of yourself, and man, it's one heck of a beautiful journey. Nostalgia hits hard for Peterson Hills University. Vishal's laughter echoing in the corridors, Anoushka's study sessions filled with shared notes and late-night talks. Those days, a whirlwind of camaraderie and knowledge, now treasured memories etched in the halls of my university journey.

I remember when I dropped the pregnancy bomb on Mumma and Papa? Classic reaction—didn't quite get the support memo. Instead, I got the boot, all for the sake of their oh-so-precious reputation. Talk about drama! But hey, I stood my ground, embraced my rebel status, and owned my decision.

It wasn't all rainbows, but those tough times? They shaped me. Who knew that becoming a rebel would be my path to independence? Life's funny that way—memory lane's a wild ride.

Jenny, my ride-or-die cousin, is like a burst of sunshine in my life. Always there for me, she's the kind of support you can't put into words. Excitement? Girl, she's more thrilled about my journey than I am! From the smallest victories to the toughest battles, Jenny's got my back. Her infectious enthusiasm is a mood lifter, turning mundane moments into joyous memories. No matter what, she's my constant, turning the ordinary into extraordinary. With Jenny by my side, every twist and turn becomes an adventure, and I'm beyond grateful for the awesome vibes she brings to my world.

Uncle and Aunty, my pillars of strength, redefine support. Through life's twists, their unwavering backing has been my constant. They handle my tantrums with grace, turning chaos into calm. Their love is a refuge, a steady anchor in the storm. Grateful for these anchors in my journey. Anupam, once a cheater, now a distant echo in my past. He missed the joy of witnessing my pregnancy, the chance to be a father. His absence, a silent blessing, allowed space for genuine love and support from those who truly matter in this incredible Journey .

And then the Rahaat saga—it's a mix of emotions, and my anxiety's hitting the roof. Guilt, worry, and a lingering sense of trauma swirl around in this whirlwind. The casual facade I put up masks the anxious mess within. Do I still need Rahaat, or am I secretly anticipating that call I might never get?

I went all tech ninja, changing my sim, and spilled the digits only to Anoushka back in Peterson Hills. It's like this girly suspense plot—did My sudden exit still affects Rahaat? The guilt about those unspoken feelings and thing we have done eats me everyday.

Picture this: a new number, a fresh chapter, but the Rahaat worry? It's like the background score to my girly, anxious saga. Like a never-ending rom-com, I'm waiting for the next twist in this crazy storyline. Maybe he's just as lost as I am in this chaotic plot, or maybe he's moved on. Either way, the uncertainty is the real star of this girly, anxious show, where I'm just trying to find my script in this unexpected drama. Holding onto faith, I mastered the art of staying mentally unattached from Peterson Hills. No more getting intoxicated—I've outgrown those days. As September bids adieu, I'm all about ending it on a hopeful note. Wish me luck for this upcoming pregnancy journey—I'm diving into it with optimism and strength.

TEN

OMG IT'S OCTOBER, ALREADY?

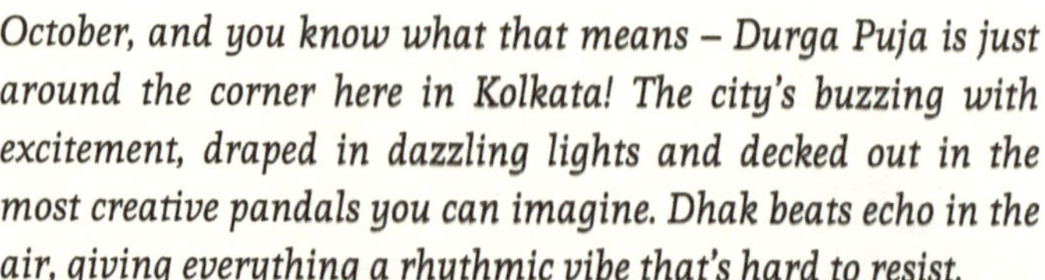

October, and you know what that means – Durga Puja is just around the corner here in Kolkata! The city's buzzing with excitement, draped in dazzling lights and decked out in the most creative pandals you can imagine. Dhak beats echo in the air, giving everything a rhythmic vibe that's hard to resist.

Meanwhile, in the midst of all this Puja madness, I'm over here, Rohini Chattopadhyay, trying to keep my cool. JSW Industries decided it's the perfect time to drop some deadlines on me. Classic, right? But hey, gotta pay the bills and keep the festive spirit alive simultaneously.

And just when I thought life couldn't get any more hectic, Anoushka swoops in with university assignments. Thanks a lot, Anoushka! But hey, we all need a little help sometimes, especially when Durga Puja and corporate chaos decide to team up against you.

So here I am, flapping through the sea of festivities, work deadlines, and assignments – because why not face all the challenges life throws at you during the most happening time in Kolkata? Cheers to Durga Puja, deadlines, and the unique chaos that is my October!

So, Puja days turn the metro into a chaotic carnival, and here I am, seven months pregnant, tackling the hustle. No other option but to ride the metro madness. It's like a daily circus, ya know? And guess what? Every time I step in, it's like cue the Bollywood soundtrack – Shah Rukh Khan's 'Jawan' on repeat in my head. Yeah, I'm one of those SRK fans. Makes the metro ride a bit less crazy, imagining I'm in some dramatic movie scene. Just a casual SRKian trying to survive the metro saga with a touch of Bollywood flair.

So there I am, innocently enjoying the metro chaos, no clue what's about to hit me. Out of nowhere, a friendly voice interrupts my thoughts, "Rohini, hey!" I turn, and there's Rahaat, strolling my way.

Panic mode activated. I contemplate my options, and what do I decide? Time to play hide and seek with my giant baby bump in this crowd. Risky move, but less risky than facing the surprise encounter with Rahaat.

Thank the metro gods, Behala station arrives like my personal savior. I rush off, and there's Uncle, my lifesaver, ready to rescue me from this unexpected social crisis. Sleep that night? Forget about it. The baby inside me decides it's the perfect time for a dance party.

Questions swirl in my head. Why is Rahaat here, and what on earth is he doing? Did Anoushka spill the beans? Traitor. The mystery unfolds in my exhausted brain as I ride off into the night, leaving the metro drama behind, but the Rahaat mystery lingers on.

Saptami hits, Durga Pujo kicks off, and guess what? Zero time for shopping. Enter Jenny, the savior, rummaging through my wardrobe like a pro. Who needs malls when you have a friend with a fashion sense, right? Aunty's on a mission, though—strictly no Pandal hopping for me. Apparently, being pregnant makes me a delicate flower in a sea of chaos.

Little does she know, Jenny and I already did a Pandal tour, courtesy of Uncle's car. Sneaky, but hey, priorities!

Fast forward to Puja in our apartment – not the grandest, but it's got that homely vibe. Missing Ranipur vibes hit me like a freight train. Ah, the memories! Puja at home is sweet, but it ain't the same without the chaos of the hometown festivities. Yarrrr, Ranipur, you're in my thoughts!

Puja sailed smoothly – no sign of Rahaat, phew! Peace prevails, shanti shanti shanti!

Now, Vijaya Dashami creeps in, a bit somber as we bid adieu to Maa Durga. Aunty dives into Sindur Khela, soaking in the festivities.

And then, a light bulb moment – "Hey Jenny! Perfect time to hit the remaining pandals!" Because, why not extend the Puja vibes a little longer? Time for some post-Dashami adventures.

The entire day unfolds as a city exploration. Visarjan postponed, replaced by a carnival a few days after Dashami – a twist in tradition. Cruising through the streets, our pitstop at Sukia Street takes an unexpected turn.

Deciding it's Fuchka o'clock, we hop out for some North Kolkata special delights. Craving that khatta meetha goodness, life's simple pleasures, right?

And then, cue the plot twist – who strolls in? None other than Mr. Rahaat! Talk about unexpected encounters. The universe has a sense of humor, especially when you're in the midst of indulging in some street food therapy.

I couldn't believe it – one moment, everything was normal, and the next, a mind-bending blur descended out of nowhere. It hit me like a tidal wave of shock, watching the world around me dissolve into chaos. Colors merged, shapes twisted, and my connection with Rahat vanished amidst the disarray. Time felt like it slipped through my fingers, leaving me bewildered in the midst of this unexpected whirlwind. The air crackled with an eerie intensity, and I stood there, utterly stunned, grappling with the surreal and bewildering spectacle that had abruptly unfolded, shattering the calm with an unforeseen jolt.

"Why'd you leave Peterson Hills?" Rahaat asked.

"Come on, dude! Remember the viva day?" I shot back.

Rahaat's face? Classic shock mode.

I needed answers, so I threw it right back at him, "How the heck did you get all my info, man?"

He brushed it off, "Doesn't matter! Just roll with me back to Peterson Hills."

"Nah, not happening," I said. And that's when Rahaat cranked up the volume, going on about this weird connection he claimed to have with me and the baby. Like, seriously? Emotions were gushing out of him, and I was left standing there feeling like I stumbled into some soap opera.

Cue my panic attack. I'm talking full-on emotional rollercoaster. Jenny swoops in, my hero, guiding me to the car. And Uncle? Silent observer in the chaos, giving me the creeps with that calm demeanor.

"Listen, there's this crazy connection between us, you, and the baby. It's like the universe planned it, missed glances, shared moments – you name it. I can't explain it, but it's deep, and it's real. I love you, and I love that baby more than anything. We're meant to be together, damn it! about that viva day... truth is, I was tangled up in my own confusion. It wasn't me; blame it on my inner demons. I was wrestling with what we had, where

it was going – all that stuff. Picture a messed-up version of me. But look, I've seen the light now. No more confusion. It's you, the baby – that's my clarity. Let's sort this out. Peterson Hills is calling, and it's not the place for my messed-up demon days. Sound good?"

That night, Rahaat's words echoed, robbing me of sleep. Tears streamed down my face, a river of emotions. Jenny, my steadfast friend, offered solace. Meanwhile, Aunty and Uncle huddled in deep discussion, undoubtedly about me and my tangled situation.

With the emotional turmoil, the pregnancy brought its own set of quirks. There's the constant battle with sleep – either the baby's kicking up a salsa party or I'm wrestling with weird dreams. Then the cravings, oh, the cravings! Pickles at midnight, anyone? And let's not forget the endless bathroom trips. It's a wild ride, and I'm just holding on, with Jenny as my sidekick and Aunty and Uncle decoding the pregnancy puzzle.

So, Aunty's throwing a Lakshmi Puja shindig, and guess who's on the guest list? Yep, Rahaat. Jenny and I, though, decided to pull a disappearing act in the name of "treatment." Smart move or major facepalm, no clue.

Coming back? It's like diving into the great unknown. Rahaat's mad as a hornet, and I bet he's gearing up for a full-on drama fest. Behind the scenes and right in front of Uncle and Aunty, brace yourself for the showdown. Life's throwing curveballs, and I'm just trying to dodge them like a pro.

ELEVEN

NOVEMBER WITH NEW HOPE

Yo, so November was a total dumpster fire, right? Jenny and I finally bounced back to the city after God-knows-what. But before that madness, had this epic phone sesh with Anoushka. Check this out:

Me: "Anoushka, spill the tea! Why'd you spill all the deets to Rahaat?"

Anoushka: "Dude, you gotta get it. You need him! The guy's head over heels for you, and come on, the kiddo needs a dad's name. Otherwise, they're stuck with the 'illegitimate child' label forever. Life's not a freakin' Bollywood feminist movie, you know?"

Me: "But seriously, spill it. Why spill everything to him?"

Anoushka: "Listen up, girl. It's not about me. It's about you and that tiny human. They deserve more than being labeled 'love child' or whatever. Rahaat's the key to avoiding that mess. It's reality check time."

As we hustled through the city mayhem, Anoushka's words echoed. November wasn't just chaos; it was this messy canvas where people are making real-life calls, juggling relationships, and dealing with society's crazy expectations. Life's a wild ride, ain't it?

Dang, Anoushka's words hitting hard, huh? Time for some serious self-reflection. Am I just on this self-centered mission to prove I'm some kind of strong, independent superhero, soaking up attention along the way? Brainstorm mode initiated.

Jenny's backing up Anoushka on this one, like, "Girl, maybe she's onto something. Are you sure you're not just caught up in this 'look at me, I'm invincible' vibe?"

But hey, let's not jump the gun. Maybe there's a deeper motive, some genuine desire to make things right. It's like a mental tug of war, torn between proving a point and doing what's truly right. November's chaos isn't just outside; it's playing out in my head too.

Guess it's time to sort through the clutter, figure out if I'm steering this ship for the right reasons or if I need to recalibrate my compass. Anoushka dropped a truth bomb, and now I'm here questioning my motives. Talk about a Reality check .

Vishal hit me up out of the blue after seven months, dropping bombs like it's a surprise party.

Vishal: "Yo, you good? How's my soon-to-be niece treating you in there?"

Me: "Yeah, she's chill. Now spill, what's the 411? Are you real! Remember those rumors?

Vishal spilled the tea .It was Shreya's drama – she's now Rohit's main squeeze, and they're both out of the gang.

Vishal: "Oh, and by the way, I'm dating Pratyasha. Big news, right? Why'd you ghost, though? Rahaat's leave from the studies scene. Any plans for a grand comeback this semester?"

My brain did somersaults trying to process all this. Shreya's a backstabber, Vishal's got a new bae, Rahaat's off the academic grid, and oh, there's a surprise baby on the way.

Me: "Wait, you and Pratyasha? Nice one. Leaving was a vibe, needed a break. Rahaat ditching studies? Unexpected. Semester plans? I need a minute to wrap my head around this, Vishal."

Jeez, it felt like I walked into a drama series without a ticket and I was just trying to keep up with the plot twists.Talk about a plot twist! Rahaat's pulling a surprise entry into the Diwali party after convincing the whole fam. Dude, I'm 8 months pregnant – can we please dial down the drama? It's like living in a reality show, and I just want a peaceful Diwali vibe, not an episode of unexpected guests and family theatrics. Let's keep it low-key, folks!

Diwali arrived with a burst of colors and festive cheer, the air alive with the crackle of fireworks and the warm glow of diyas. Amidst the celebration, Aunty, concerned for my pregnancy, strictly banned me from the fiery revelry. Just when the night seemed settled, Rahaat made a surprise entrance, showering Uncle and Aunty with sweetness. Even skeptical Jenny was won over. Diwali's magic unfolded not only in the dazzling lights but in the unexpected harmony that embraced us, turning a night of caution into a celebration of togetherness.

Aloha! dinner's served, and guess who's on the guest list? Rahaat, of course. Not feeling the whole eating vibe lately, but Aunty's like, 'It's cool, happens.' Post-dinner, Uncle's all, 'Balcony chat with Rahaat, just for kicks.' Seriously, can't a balcony just be a balcony? Casual evening turning into a mystery novel, I Swear.In the dimly lit balcony emotions ran high as Rahaat confronted me.

Me: So, like, why did you show up out of nowhere?

Rahaat: I was missing the drama, obviously. Why'd you ghost me? Left Peterson Hills like it's no big deal.

Me: Uh, hello? None of your business.

Rahaat: Totally is!

Me: Remember viva day? You were off with Hiya Banerjee and Kankhita Sen, leaving me hanging!

Rahaat, looking like he just ran a marathon, tried to keep his cool.

Me: That hit me hard, and what's with the hanky panky at my place? You were just there to take advantage of my vulnerable situation. Get lost, I yelled!

Rahaat, officially in Furious Mode, tried to play the defender.

Rahaat: How does leaving studies and joining a job help me take advantage of your vulnerable situation? I was clueless, just trying to secure our future. Yes, you, me, and our cute little munchkin.

I threw some sassy punches his way.

Me: Did I ask for that? No! Then why, Rahaat? Just let me have some peace. I've been through enough.

Rahaat, in a fit of passion, shot back. "Cause that's MY BABY! I don't give a damn who Anupam is; I just know that you guys are my responsibility."

So, there we were, finally finding some clarity in the chaos named Rahaat. About to lock lips when, bam! Labor hits me like a freight train – not a false alarm, but the real deal.

Cue the rush, like, hospital rush, delivery room rush. I'm gripping Rahaat's hand for dear life, and in the midst of the chaos, there's Jenny Uncle, Aunty – everyone just blending into the madness.

As the darkness starts closing in, Rahaat's voice echoes. "Tried so damn hard to be your everything, Best Girl Dad ever. Loved you since day one. I don't wanna lose my best friend, but things went haywire that day at your place. Anoushka pulled some hero moves to track you down." His words fading into the background.

And then, amid all the emotional upheaval, a tiny cry breaks through. That's my baby – my girl. I named her RATRI, because, you know, she made quite the entrance. A night to remember, bringing with it a flood of emotions, love, and the unbreakable bond between Rahaat, Ratri, and yours truly.

TWELVE

DYNAMIC DECEMBER

Chillin' in Peterson Hills on December 25th, braving the cold, but who cares? Fam's back together, Rahaat's on board, and Ratri's bringing all the sweetness. Started up something new – just rollin' with it. The weather might be frosty, but inside, it's all warm vibes, you know? It's not just about being home; it's about cooking up dreams with the crew. So, here's to the holidays, startup adventures, and the cozy chaos that makes Peterson Hills feel like the place to be. Cheers to family, warmth, and whatever this new chapter brings! After Ratri's premature arrival, the joy of her birth was tempered by the reality of the NICU. Each passing moment felt like an eternity, my heart echoing the beeps of the monitors that surrounded her tiny form. Worry wrapped around me like a heavy blanket as I watched the delicate dance of medical professionals tending to her. The fragility of her early existence intensified every emotion – from the elation of becoming a parent to the fear that gripped my soul. The NICU became a realm of hope and anxiety, where each small victory felt monumental, and each setback felt like a storm.

In the NICU, Rahaat was my rock, a constant support during Ratri's premature birth. His reassuring presence turned the sterile hospital room into a haven of strength. Together, we weathered the uncertainty, finding comfort in shared glances and silent understanding. In those challenging moments, his unwavering support became the anchor that steadied my worries.

Becoming a new mom brought a whirlwind of emotions – overwhelming love, joy, and a touch of apprehension. My little angel, Ratri, embodied perfection in every tiny feature. Her delicate fingers curled around mine, and her eyes sparkled with an innocence that melted my heart. Pure love in miniature form.

After three weeks, the hospital finally released Ratri. Relief washed over us like a soothing tide. Jenny, Uncle, Aunty, Rahaat, and, of course, I couldn't contain our happiness. The house echoed with laughter and celebration, a symphony of joy as we embraced our little miracle returning home.

We waved goodbye to Jenny, Uncle, and Aunty, and suddenly it hit me—I left my job. Crazy, right? But here's the deal: underneath the "OMG, I'm jobless" drama, there's this buzz of excitement. Why? 'Cause I'm diving into the whole family-making thing.

Marriage? Well, let's just say our plans got lost in the whirlwind. No biggie, though. Life's a merry-go-round , and we're just along for the ride.

Now, here's the tea: my fam ghosted me. Silence. Crickets. It stung, but guess what? Rahaat's got no fam drama either. Zilch. Nada. It's just us three against the world. Like, who needs a script when you can freestyle, right?

So, in this wild ride called life, we're winging it. Rahaat, Ratri, and me, creating our own version of family vibes. No rulebook, just a whole lot of love and Netflix nights.

Sure, there are bumps, but our trio? Unbreakable. Our story? Still unfolding. Call it unconventional, call it girly chaos – either way, it's ours. And in this cozy little haven we've built, the world can keep spinning. Cheers to love, laughter, and navigating this girl-boss life with my ride-or-dies!

So, picture this: I'm in the baby-sitting wilderness, clueless as it gets. Enter Chaitali Aunty, the magical Marry Poppins,Anoushka's Mom who swoops in like a parenting guru. Suddenly, my munchkin Ratri's got a full-on squad – a Granny, a bunch of Uncles and Aunties, and, oh yeah, the awesome couple who birthed her into this world.

But here's the kicker: Rahaat? That guy's not just a dad; he's a legit awesome dad. Diapers, midnight feeds, the whole shebang – he's all in. It's like watching a superhero origin story, but in dad mode.

With this crew, parenting feels like a tag-team wrestling match, minus the spandex. Chaitali Aunty drops the wisdom bombs, Granny brings in the timeless classics, and Rahaat? Well, he's the cool dad, effortlessly handling baby duties like a pro.

Grateful doesn't even cover it. Ratri's got this whole tribe looking out for her, and I'm just here soaking up the parenting hacks like a sponge. Who knew baby-sitting chaos could turn into a heartwarming saga with this epic support crew? Here's to the village it takes to raise a munchkin – and I'm living right in the heart of it.

So, Rahaat and I are in this epic battle over Ratri's last name. I'm all about that Chattopadhyay life – sounds way cooler than D'Souza, right? But let's hit pause on the name game because reality check – I'm still grinding through the student life at Peterson Hills University.

Thank the stars, the exams got a winter vacation delay. So, February's first week is now the battlefield for my academic showdown. It's this weird mix of surname debates and cramming sessions. Chattopadhyay might sound sophisticated, but mastering those textbooks is a whole different saga.

Picture this: me, Rahaat, and a pile of books – the unholy trinity of pre-exam chaos. Forget the surname spat; it's all about surviving the academic rollercoaster while dreaming of a chill winter break. And Ofcourse My little Cupcake.Thank God Chaitali Aunty is with us.

So, our place turned into this buzzing hub today.It's a Cute Christmas get together Vishal, Pratyasha, Ahaan, Firdausi, and the one and only Anoushka – our resident matchmaker who's still rocking the single life. Note to self: convince her to get a boyfriend, like, ASAP.

University gossip is like a daily soap starring Vishal, Firdausi, Anoushka, Pratyasha, and Ahaan. The tea is hot – Rohit ditched Shreya, cue the drama! Juniors are the unsung heroes, stirring the rumor pot with epic tales. Class secrets, teacher gossips – it's like our own little reality show. Vishal's the storyteller, Firdausi's the detective, Anoushka's the matchmaker, Pratyasha's the drama queen, and Ahaan's the silent observer. Together, they turn mundane lectures into juicy plotlines. Who needs Netflix when you've got the university grapevine?

But here's the kicker – the excitement meter isn't exactly pointing my way. It's all Ratri, Ratri, Ratri. I get it, she's adorable, but hey, "Does anyone want to chat with me too?" Feeling a bit like the side character in my own story.

Anoushka's on her mission, slyly matchmaking between bites of snacks. The crew's more invested in Ratri's coos than my attempts at conversation. I'm waving the "Hey, I'm here too" flag, but Ratri's stealing the spotlight like a little superstar.

In the midst of baby talk and matchmaking schemes, I'm drawing the fine line between hosting duties and wanting a slice of the attention pie. Parenthood reality check: sometimes you play second fiddle, even at your own gathering. Here's to hoping they remember I exist when the baby cuteness wears off.

Rahaat totally owns the dad game, stealing the spotlight at our little shindig. He's the life of the party, doing the baby daddy dance like a champ. Meanwhile, I'm in the background, low-key craving some attention. But hey, it's all good 'cause seeing my fam together rocks.

In the middle of the baby giggles and the chaos, Rahaat's like a ninja partner – rocking both dad and boyfriend duties effortlessly. He's the MVP, turning the ordinary into a low-key awesome day. Here's to Rahaat, the laid-back superhero of our family hangouts!

On the eve of the 31st, anticipation hung in the air as I sat on Rohini's balcony, closing the pages of her diary. Dinner was a promise waiting to be fulfilled after Rahaat's return from the office. Ratri, the little one, had succumbed to the lull of sleep, leaving Rohini engrossed in her semester preparations.

As I delved into the intimate details of Rohini's life, a portrait of resilience emerged. At just 24 years old, she navigated the challenges of pregnancy alone, facing each obstacle with grace and determination. Her strength was a beacon, a testament that age was no barricade against life's unexpected turns. The echoes of pages turned carried the weight of her journey, and I marveled at the fortitude she displayed.

Then there was Rahaat, a constant presence in Rohini's life, a steady force except for a hiccup in July. Through the diary's narrative, I detailed his unwavering support—a pillar for Rohini through thick and thin. Despite the glitches of July, Rahaat's commitment never wavered, showcasing a love and dedication that transcended ordinary bounds.

Lost in contemplation, I was oblivious to Rohini's approach until she stood beside me. A hug enveloped us, and with a genuine smile, she uttered a heartfelt "Thank you." Gratitude infused her words, and in that moment, I felt the profound impact of witnessing their story unfold. The narrative of courage, love, and fath in the air, bouquet of shared moments.

As the clock ticked closer to midnight, I found myself grateful to be part of their narrative. Whispering my thanks to the universe for choosing me as a character in their extraordinary tale, I realized that the 31st night was not merely a countdown to the new year but a celebration of the strength found in unexpected places, the unwavering support of companions like Rahaat, and the indomitable spirit of Rohini, who faced life's storms with a courage that left an indelible mark on those fortunate enough to witness it.

Rohini reacher her happily ever after because I let her do so. But Girls and Guys do not try this at home. Your life isn't a part of Dramabaaz Daily Soap, Hindi Serials, web series or my story.